Ghost Story

Mark Ravenhill

A Samuel French Acting Edition

SAMUEL FRENCH

FOUNDED 1830

SAMUELFRENCH.COM
SAMUELFRENCH-LONDON.CO.UK

GHOST STORY was first produced as part of the Sky Arts Playhouse: Live project. The performance was directed by Mark Ravenhill. The cast was as follows:

MERYL . . . . Lesley Manville

LISA . . . . Juliet Stevenson

HANNAH . . . . Lyndsey Marshal

CHARACTERS

MERYL

LISA

HANNAH

(**MERYL** *and* **LISA.**)

LISA. Have you ever…?

MERYL. This isn't about me.

LISA. But… I wondered…how you came to –

MERYL. This is about you.

LISA. Did you ever…did you heal yourself…did you?

MERYL. That would be crossing the line.

LISA. But your understanding comes from…you understand illness because…?

MERYL. I'm a healer. That's all –

LISA. I understand.

MERYL. That's all I – Of course you are asking questions: Who is this woman? Is she like me? Do I see myself in this woman?

LISA. Yes.

MERYL. Do I trust this woman?

LISA. Maybe.

MERYL. All of these questions are natural. Natural questions. But that is not the task. We are here to work on you. You will be healed. Where is your anger?

LISA. Everywhere.

MERYL. Illness is anger. Anger caught in the body, a trapped anger. Are you angry with yourself?

LISA. Yes.

MERYL. Then let's start with that. If you can forgive yourself… I guide. But it's not for me to forgive you. It's for you…here. All the work you do, you do on yourself.

LISA. *(to mirror)* I…

MERYL. Do you see a woman you can forgive?

LISA. I…look so ill.

MERYL. Is that what you see?

LISA. Skin yellowed. Gums rotting. Patches where hair should be.

MERYL. You're a beautiful woman.

LISA. Everything falling away and I see a skull.

MERYL. We see what we tell ourselves to see. Forgive yourself.

LISA. I'm so frightened.

MERYL. What's your fear? Name it.

LISA. No.

MERYL. Tell me what you think of me.

LISA. Well…

MERYL. You can't access those feelings.

LISA. No, I can't access those feelings.

MERYL. Words create a story about ourselves. I'm a person who is dying. I have no choice. My body is diseased and ugly. My breast is my enemy. Is that a story you can hear in your head?

LISA. Yes.

MERYL. So. A new voice, a new… I'm at the centre of my universe, I am filled with love, my body is filled with well-being. We can…if we do the work. Will you do the work?

LISA. I'll try.

MERYL. Alright. Now. You look at me and you don't have the words to describe what you feel.

LISA. You're a guide. You're a healer. You're a wise woman.

MERYL. I'm going to ask you to draw me.

LISA. Alright.

MERYL. But…the crayon in the other hand. So now you're not controlling with your conscious…you see?

LISA. I see.

MERYL. I'm going to count down from twenty and the picture will be done. It's an image, an instant picture of what's in your…here we go. Twenty…nineteen…

eighteen…seventeen…sixteen…fifteen…fourteen…thirteen…twelve…eleven…ten…nine…eight…seven…six…five…four…three…two…one. And – stop. What do you see?

LISA. I…

MERYL. Would you like to show me…?

LISA. …

MERYL. There are no judgments. No punishments.

> (**LISA** *hands* **MERYL** *the picture.*)

LISA. I can't draw.

MERYL. I look like the wicked witch don't I? Would you describe that as…?

LISA. A witch. It's yes.

MERYL. Isn't that interesting? Here I am the healer but I'm also the witch. That's interesting. I would have been burnt. Maybe in a previous life I was. Maybe they pulled me into the market place and they accused me… Somebody pointed at me, somebody – maybe someone like you – pointed at me and said: You live without a man, you have your own thoughts and your own space and you tell women that they can love their bodies, that their breasts are not their enemies and so we say that you should be burnt.

LISA. I'm not doing that. I'm diseased. I want to be well. I want to heal. I want to work with you.

MERYL. You are angry with me. That's only right. Someone else has to be the focus of your anger. I'm in the room. I'm used to this. It's part of the process. You hate me but –

LISA. No.

> (**LISA** *holds up the picture.*)

This is nothing.

> (**LISA** *rips up the picture.*)

I am diseased. My breast was removed. I have forgiven the man, the surgeon who ripped and maimed me. He did the best he could with the knowledge he had at the time. My scarring is terrible. But I look at it now and I can see the beauty there. Yes, I cover it with this prosthetic but I can love my scar. There have been two wonderful years since my operation. My daughter had her first kiss from a boy. My husband lost twenty pounds and we have – sometimes – reassumed intimacy. But now. It's in my lung. They've found a spot, my lung. You see? It's back.

MERYL. I see.

LISA. I did all the work on myself once and now…

MERYL. It's back and…

LISA. And I'm overwhelmed by darkness. The story I'm living is… I will move closer and closer to my death. It will be a horrible death. I will lose control of my body. I will be in great pain. I need a helper to change that story. I need you.

MERYL. Then we'll work together.

LISA. I'm sorry I want to know if you've ever –

MERYL. Of course you do but –

LISA. I want to know if – if we're going on this journey – what's your experience of – are you a survivor…do you…?

MERYL. I can't cross the line.

LISA. Because…?

MERYL. Because one person must be the healer. You want to be well –

LISA. Yes…

MERYL. And it won't work – I can't empower you to release your anger if I'm also – do you see?

LISA. I just want to –

MERYL. Talk to your fear. Tell her what you're feeling. I'm your fear. Talk to me. Name me. Give me a name.

LISA. You…

MERYL. What's happening?

LISA. I can't.

MERYL. Are you ending the session?

LISA. I just can't do that.

MERYL. Are you leaving and going back to your partner and your tests and – are you ending the work with me?

LISA. I don't know.

MERYL. You want me to tell you about myself. But I can't do that. I can't… I understand your journey. I share your feelings. I… I want us to do this work together.

LISA. Because?

MERYL. Because you're a brave, beautiful woman who can be well again.

LISA. I don't want to go. But…going on. I am so worn down by fear and Western medicine.

MERYL. Look at this room. Look around. Look at me. Look at my hand. Does any of this actually exist? Actually objectively exist? No. It only exists in my perception. The universe is only as I perceive it to be. I am ill. I am well. I decide.

LISA. But still…the…

MERYL. Say the word.

LISA. Cancer.

MERYL. Louder.

LISA. Cancer.

MERYL. Draw it for me. The cancer. As you see it.

> (**MERYL** *gives* **LISA** *a chalk.*)

On the wall.

LISA. On the…? *(laughs)*

MERYL. *(laughs)* I know isn't it crazy?

> (*As* **LISA** *draws on the wall:*)

Start with the eyes. That's good. I'm seeing a lot of anger there. But also fear. Could the cancer be as frightened of you as you are of it?

Now the mouth. So…it's hungry. It's desperate to eat which means…it's needy, it's weak.

MERYL. *(cont.)* And a body. A shape, form. What's the size of the creature?

So it's big, bigger than you. And it's reaching out to you.

Is it a man or a woman?

> (**LISA** *draws a primitive penis on the cancer, like a cave drawing.*)

So it's a very male energy. There's a male who is big and he's hungry and he's reaching out to you and he's going to eat you. Is this how it seems to you?

LISA. Yes – that's it.

MERYL. Now then speak to it. Tell it what you feel.

LISA. Could you leave me alone please. Could you go away. I'm not ready for you. You see, my daughter still needs me. She doesn't know enough about the world. I still want to guide her. And my bloke. He really loves me. He'll go to bits if I let him down. I'll let him down if I go and I don't want to do that.

MERYL. But I can take you. You won't be missed. Your bloke. Your daughter. You're telling me they're the special ones. So I can take you.

LISA. I'm special.

MERYL. How are you special?

LISA. I'm working on myself. Every day I'm making myself grow a bit more. Because I'm unique. Because…

MERYL. That's it. That's good. Now if you –

LISA. No.

MERYL. No?

LISA. I'm not doing this. This is…

MERYL. Yes?

LISA. I don't believe this. They're not my words. They're words to please you. I'm just the same as everyone else. I've never done anything special in my life. I was born in a little house that looked just the same as a thousand other little houses. I went to a school and I wore the uniform and I was average at everything. Now I work in a little cubicle that's just the same as a hundred other cubicles on the seventh floor which is just the same as every other floor. And I've been happy with that. It's been okay. It's been good. I've never wanted to be special. And now I've got breast cancer and it's spread into my lung. And that's not special or dramatic or – It's boring actually boring. And all the other women – the lines of them sitting there waiting for their chemo and their radio and wearing headscarves and their wigs. Lots of them think they're special. Fighting the fight. But it doesn't make it better. It doesn't –

MERYL. I have seen miracles.

(*LISA gets her coat and bag, prepares to leave.*)

LISA. I'm sorry. I've wasted your time.

MERYL. It's our time.

LISA. I'll pay you.

MERYL. There's no need.

LISA. This is my choice. I want you to have the money.

MERYL. I don't want to take the money.

LISA. I'm just paying you for your time.

MERYL. Take it.

> (**MERYL** *pushes the money on the floor.* **LISA** *gets down to pick up the money which is scattered about the floor.* **MERYL** *moves over and forms the shape of the cancer drawn on the wall.*)

Please. I need you. I'm hungry. I need to eat.

LISA. Don't.

MERYL. Because I'm big, because I'm male, all this male energy then I frighten you.

LISA. This is a stupid game.

MERYL. But I need a woman. To feed on, to eat. I've already taken your breast. I've taken your breast and I fed on that and it kept me happy for months. But now I'm back and there's so much more of you. I can taste your lung…your lung tastes good. Maybe I'll take that next. Please. If you don't stop me. I'm so hungry. I can't help myself if you don't do anything, if you walk away then I will spread through your lymphs and that will take me round your whole body and I will eat everything, I will eat you all away. Destroy you.

LISA. Leave me alone.

MERYL. I want your body. I want to take you. We belong together. I own you.

LISA. Stop this no stop. I will not... My cancer's not like that. Don't tell me what my cancer is like. It's my cancer. You can't see it. They look at it on scans and pictures. They look at bits of me under their microscopes. They show me bits of myself and tell me what it is. But this cancer is mine. Somedays my cancer is hurting me and scaring me, yes. Somedays my cancer is the bully in the playground or or or the headmaster. But somedays cancer is my lover. Somedays we're alone together, shut away in the afternoon and we sleep and we whisper together. My cancer knows my body better than any man has ever... So please don't... You can't be my cancer, it's too...special,

MERYL. You've turned the corner.

LISA. You think so?

MERYL. I can never tell when it will come, which session. But I know it when it happens.

LISA. What comes? What happens?

MERYL. Something has been released. You've moved on. You're going to be well. Can you feel that?

LISA. I don't know.

MERYL. Pick up the mirror. What do you see?

(**LISA** *looks in the mirror.*)

LISA. A bit better.

MERYL. And forgive yourself.

LISA. I ...for... I fff...

MERYL. That's it. Cry now. It's a release.

LISA. I won't forget this

MERYL. I'm a Survivor.

LISA. Yes.

MERYL. I had cancer, my breast was... But I did the work on myself and...

LISA. I knew that. I sensed.

MERYL. I shouldn't cross the line but...

LISA. I want to be like you.

MERYL. Like me?

LISA. Well and happy. Like you. Happy and well.

MERYL. You can be.

LISA. You promise?

MERYL. I...

LISA. No. I understand. You can't promise. I can see that. But I need to know. I don't want to be an ill person.

MERYL. We'll meet once a week. You'll do the work on yourself.

LISA. I will. Yes.

MERYL. And as we let out the negative thoughts, new positive thoughts will flow through you and...

LISA. I'll be well. I understand it's a long journey but that little bit of light to... I lied to you. My husband. My husband hasn't... He's a good man. But this thing...my husband sleeps on the sofa.

MERYL. I see.

LISA. And I wonder if you could just hold me for...?

MERYL. Of course.

(**MERYL** *holds* **LISA**.)

LISA. Thank you very much. That's good isn't it? The work's beginning.

(**HANNAH** *with shopping*.)

HANNAH. There was a woman in front of me. And there was one last butternut squash left and this woman took the butternut squash. And I felt this great surge of anger. 'That's my butternut squash for the butternut squash soup I am going to prepare tonight for my girlfriend and you've taken the butternut squash you bitch, bitch.' Wasn't that ridiculous? But then I laughed at myself and I said "Ridiculous,' and I got a pumpkin instead and do you know actually it's Halloween today so everything's worked out for the best because it's Halloween and we're going to be eating pumpkin soup. So really the woman who took the butternut squash was doing us a favour. I love you.

MERYL. I love you too.

HANNAH. There's something wrong.

MERYL. No.

HANNAH. One of the kids called me Nan today. I've had Mum before. But. I realised I'm very frightened of becoming an older woman. How was your day? Did you have a bad day?

MERYL. No. Everything's ok. Really I'm –

HANNAH. I don't believe you.

MERYL. Well –

HANNAH. Maybe once we've eaten.

MERYL. Yes.

HANNAH. Come here. My beautiful bird. Let me hold you.

(*They hold each other.*)

There's no intimacy here.

MERYL. Really?

HANNAH. This is supposed to be you and me –

MERYL. I know.

HANNAH. We promised. At the end of the day we leave everything behind and everyone else and it's just you and me.

MERYL. It is.

HANNAH. You and me together alone and –

MERYL. We are, we are.

HANNAH. You're somewhere else.

MERYL. I love you.

HANNAH. Yes?

MERYL. Yes. Of course yes. Yes I love you. You're very beautiful and you have an incredible aura and I love you.

(**MERYL** *and* **HANNAH** *kiss.*)

LISA. It's like a battle isn't it? And suddenly I can feel it. The battle's turning and all my fighters – like my immune system – they're suddenly going out and they are fighting the cancer which is brilliant. Because once I've got the strength. Once my mind is telling them go out and fight the cancer then I'm invincible aren't I? Nothing can beat that. Nothing can beat me now.

MERYL. How was that?

HANNAH. You're still… You're not actually here with me.

MERYL. Of course I am of course I –

HANNAH. No.

MERYL. What do you – what do you want me to do?

HANNAH. I just feel…

MERYL. Cut myself? Is that the proof that you – ?

HANNAH. No no no.

MERYL. Because I love I love you I love you and if that's not – if you can't hear that then –

HANNAH. I'm hearing the words.

MERYL. Then really you should look at yourself – at your own insecurities if you can't then –

HANNAH. I know all my insecurities and I acknowledge them but –

MERYL. Then please just allow us to be.

HANNAH. Would you like a rub?

MERYL. That would be good.

(**HANNAH** *rubs* **MERYL.**)

I'm sorry it's hurting.

HANNAH. Would you like me to stop?

MERYL. Yes I would actually. I'm sorry that's just what I – yes
    I would. I would like you to stop.

HANNAH. Alright then.

    Who is it?

    Who's in this space?

MERYL. I don't know.

HANNAH. Somebody else in this space. I can only see me
    and I can see you. But you…

MERYL. No.

HANNAH. There's someone else in this space with you.

MERYL. You're young.

HANNAH. Don't patronise me.

MERYL. You don't know.

HANNAH. Who?

MERYL. Lots of… Mum. Dad. Lovers. They're all in here
    chatting away all the time.

HANNAH. Not for me.

MERYL. Because you're younger, but as you get older –

HANNAH. I'm your lover not your child. There's…
    A negative energy. I can feel –

MERYL. Yes.

HANNAH. If I'm here I can feel a negative energy.

MERYL. A client.

HANNAH. Ah.

MERYL. Last week.

HANNAH. And there's still…?

MERYL. She was very strong. She brought a lot of negative –

HANNAH. You have to let this go. If we're going to –

MERYL. I do.

HANNAH. But still –

MERYL. This one woman I – I crossed a line with this one
    woman.

HANNAH. I see.

MERYL. She was a cancer woman.

HANNAH. I see.

MERYL. And I – you know – there are plenty of cancer women but this woman, I… She had a breast cancer and the breast had been removed and so it –

HANNAH. You connected with that.

MERYL. I did. It was my case. It was me.

HANNAH. But she's not you.

MERYL. No. She was another woman but her story was my story.

HANNAH. Did she have a beautiful young girlfriend who was giving her pumpkin soup for Halloween?

MERYL. No. She had a man and a child.

HANNAH. There we are.

MERYL. But otherwise –

HANNAH. Lots of women have cancer. Their breast is removed. They survive.

MERYL. It was like me if I had followed another life path.

HANNAH. But you fought it. You're special.

MERYL. I could have been there with the job and the man and –

HANNAH. But you met me. And you cured yourself.

MERYL. I did. Met you and I cured myself.

HANNAH. Where is she?

MERYL. She's gone now.

HANNAH. I don't believe you.

MERYL. Come on. Let's relax.

HANNAH. Point to her in the room.

MERYL. She's there.

HANNAH. And what's she doing?

MERYL. She's crying. But in a way…that's releasing, that's…

HANNAH. Ask her to leave.

MERYL. There's no need.

HANNAH. Tell her that it's a special time/ our time, and you want her to go now.

MERYL. There really is no need for that.

HANNAH. Are you frightened? She's a woman. She's a client. She pays sixty pounds. It's a transaction. You allow her to do the work on herself. Say to her, tell her...

MERYL. *(to LISA)* I feel like you're me.

LISA. Yes?

MERYL. I'm sorry if I've crossed a line but I really feel you're me.

LISA. That's alright.

MERYL. All those things...the school the house the job the fella I had all those things.

LISA. I see.

MERYL. But... I had the cancer. A man, a surgeon he tore off my breast just as...

LISA. Oh.

MERYL. They say it's necessary, these men they tell us it's necessary to chop at our bodies but I'm not convinced...

LISA. Do you know really I...

MERYL. And I have a prosthetic there was remission but then my lung...

LISA. Please.

MERYL. So our stories you see are so...identical.

LISA. I'm sorry if this is hard or cruel yes this is hard and but...

MERYL. Yes?

LISA. I don't really want to hear that.

MERYL. I'm sorry.

LISA. Because now that I've actually released this incredible energy –

MERYL. Alright then.

LISA. I really need – I'm sorry – to be surrounded by positive –

MERYL. No.

LISA. I need this time for positive thoughts – I need to attract well-being to myself – I'm at a stage where if I'm with too much negative –

MERYL. I understand.

LISA. I suppose I'm frightened that I'll be overwhelmed by all your negative – when what I'm filled with is a positive –

MERYL. I can see.

LISA. That was your past. Your experience that was your past. So let it go – just –

MERYL. Of course.

LISA. You have to work to let that go.

MERYL. I'll make the soup with you.

HANNAH. You haven't said goodbye to her yet.

MERYL. There's no need.

HANNAH. I think you should.

MERYL. I really don't –

You're going to be well. I feel that very strongly.

LISA. So do I.

MERYL. We've done the work.

LISA. Of course.

LISA. I feel bad now.

MERYL. There's no need.

LISA. You've got the same story as me.

MERYL. It wasn't part of our deal. I crossed the line.

LISA. You wanted to tell me about –

MERYL. Not now –

LISA. I'm a survivor. You're a survivor. We should –

MERYL. You've got your bloke and your girl waiting for you at home.

LISA. We can share our stories.

MERYL. You cook them a lovely meal and tell them that Mummy is going to be well again.

LISA. It came back on your lung and –

MERYL. I was wrong to tell you about that.

LISA. When it came back on your lung. How did you fight that?

MERYL. My story is not your story. I'm the healer.

LISA. But you're well now?

MERYL. I crossed the line once but I'm not crossing it again. Goodbye.

LISA. I want to know that you're alright.

MERYL. I'm well. I'm strong. Goodbye.

HANNAH. That's it. Say goodbye.

LISA. You don't want this in your lovely room. *[the drawing on the wall]*

MERYL. I can do it later.

LISA. I want to do it.

MERYL. I don't want you to do it.

LISA. But I want to do it.

(**LISA** *begins to wash the wall*)

HANNAH. Is she gone now?

MERYL. All gone.

HANNAH. The room's a lot lighter now isn't it?

MERYL. Much lighter.

HANNAH. *(sits)* So she was sat here crying but she's gone now? You have a wonderful gift. You've healed so many people. And you've healed yourself. You are such an incredible woman. I can't believe I met a woman as incredible as you.

LISA. Have you got someone?

MERYL. It doesn't matter.

LISA. But there's someone to look after you?

MERYL. That's crossing the line.

LISA. I know but I just want to…there's someone you can talk to? In the evenings when you go home and you've been healing. There's a man?

MERYL. No.

LISA. Oh.

MERYL. There was a man and a kid. I had a man called Harry and a daughter called Lily. But I left them.

LISA. I see.

MERYL. My choice.

LISA. Are you happy?

MERYL. This is all about me.

LISA. Have you got someone else now?

MERYL. Let's not talk about me.

LISA. I'd just like to know if there's someone else.

MERYL. No.

LISA. Oh.

MERYL. I'm alone. But I like that. It's very quiet. It's very calm. I just cook myself some soup and sit here in this room on my own and I think.

LISA. So long as you're happy.

MERYL. It's very important: learning to be happy by yourself.

HANNAH. What are you thinking about?

MERYL. I'm thinking about how much I love you.

HANNAH. Well that's good because I'm thinking about how much I love you.

MERYL. *(laugh)* That's good.

HANNAH. I couldn't bear to be alone. Even if you're gone for a day I can't stand to be here without you. I can't remember what my life was like without you.

MERYL. You were alright. You were happy.

HANNAH. Not like this. And now that you're here. I want you to be here always and forever.

MERYL. But you could be happy on your own.

HANNAH. Never.

MERYL. Never?

HANNAH. Never.

MERYL. Listen…

HANNAH. I want this moment never to stop.

MERYL. It…

HANNAH. What?

MERYL. It's come back.

HANNAH. What has?

LISA. Just this one last bit.

MERYL. I went for a check up a few weeks ago.

HANNAH. You didn't say anything about that.

MERYL. It was a routine, I've been so well…

HANNAH. Why didn't you tell me?

MERYL. It was such a routine thing. I forgot about it myself. I only found the letter in a drawer the night before. You were working on your lesson plans so I didn't say anything.

HANNAH. I thought you were always going to tell me.

MERYL. I was but it was so routine and you were so busy so I just popped in because I really thought it was going to be such a routine…

LISA. There's always one stubborn bit.

MERYL. But that's when they told me you see that it's in my lung now. Really quite aggressively.

HANNAH. You knew this…?

MERYL. A few weeks ago.

HANNAH. Did you phone Harry?

MERYL. I did actually.

HANNAH. Oh.

MERYL. Because of Lily. I wanted him to know because of Lily it's important that he knows.

HANNAH. I can have a kid.

MERYL. It just gives him time to prepare Lily for the worst.

HANNAH. I want to have a kid. My body's ready for that. Shall we have a kid?

MERYL. I've decided not to have any radio and chemo.

HANNAH. Ever?

MERYL. Ever.

HANNAH. Why?

MERYL. Because what is that going to do? Chemo? Radio? What can they do? They can put a stop to it for a while…they can slow it down…but if they can't fight the cause…if you can't find the cause then what's the…?

HANNAH. What's the cause?

MERYL. Anger.

HANNAH. But you've been working on –

MERYL. There's still more there. I've got to work on that. I've got to find every last bit of anger and I've got to let it out of me.

HANNAH. But alongside the chemo and the –

MERYL. No. No. Just me now. Just me fighting this.

HANNAH. And me.

We're working together.

MERYL. We can't. This is mine.

HANNAH. But I'm your partner.

MERYL. You don't know – this is my battle – no doctor – no –

HANNAH. I love you.

MERYL. I'm sorry but you're a child –

HANNAH. I am not – You want to be alone?

MERYL. I do. Yes. Me. Alone. In this room. Anyone else will…hold me back.

HANNAH. You don't love me?

MERYL. I haven't got time for that. I can't –

HANNAH. You don't love me.

MERYL. Illness. Death. These are selfish things.

HANNAH. Would you like me to leave?

MERYL. This is about my anger.

LISA. I'm sorry. I wasn't expecting you. Is there another woman who…?

HANNAH. No there's no-one else.

LISA. You're on your own here?

HANNAH. I am yes I'm on my own here.

LISA. Oh I'm sorry I thought… I was looking for another
    woman, for Meryl. I came to see her last year and I
    wanted to…

HANNAH. Meryl isn't here.

LISA. Can I leave her a note? If I scribble something and –

HANNAH. How well did you know Meryl?

LISA. A little. She –

HANNAH. Meryl passed away.

LISA. Oh.

HANNAH. After a very long battle. Don't be sad. It was a
    very spiritual moment. I was with her. I was travelling.
    I'd gone to Thailand. But my name was on the form. I
    flew back. I went to the hospital. I held her hand. I was
    very privileged. I saw her spirit leave her body.

LISA. Sorry I just… I was so sure she'd be here and now to
    find –

HANNAH. Everything moves on.

LISA. Was it cancer?

HANNAH. Yes her breast then her lymphs then her lung
    and then all over.

LISA. I thought… I knew she had… But she was so strong.
    She was a great healer. Are you her daughter?

HANNAH. I was her partner.

LISA. Oh.

HANNAH. You seem surprised. Did you think she was on
    her own?

LISA. It was over a year ago I don't remember.

HANNAH. Did she tell you she had a partner?

LISA. That would have been crossing the line.

HANNAH. I know but still…

LISA. I was a woman with cancer and she was my healer
    and so anything else would have been crossing the line.

HANNAH. I suppose.

LISA. But actually…

HANNAH. Yes?

LISA. Actually… There was a moment. I'd drawn on the wall here. With a piece of chalk and then I was leaving and I looked at it and it looked so terrible I just wanted it to go I wanted to clean it up.

HANNAH. She would've done that.

LISA. I know she would've but somehow for me you know I really felt like I'd turned a corner and I didn't want to leave that thing on the wall.

HANNAH. Okay.

LISA. So I decided to stay here and clean it up. And that's when I crossed the line.

HANNAH. I see.

LISA. Because I had this sense… I don't know why but I had this feeling… I just had this feeling that this wasn't just my story but that it was her story.

HANNAH. She would have known by then. It was in her lung. She came home and told me straight away. I made her soup and we cried together.

LISA. I crossed the line and I pushed her: Do you know about this? Are you going through this too?

HANNAH. She wouldn't cross the line.

LISA. No. She was a healer. She wasn't going to cross the line. And so I said to her. Alright. Just tell me one thing. At home, tonight, is there someone? And she said yes, she could go home in the evening and there you would be cooking her a soup and that made her very happy.

HANNAH. That's good.

LISA. So I was able to leave here much lighter because I knew, you see, that she wasn't on her own. When did she die?

HANNAH. Last summer.

LISA. I thought she was going to make it.

HANNAH. So did I.

LISA. I mean how can that be? How can I fight and win and she can lose? It doesn't make sense.

HANNAH. Why did you come?

LISA. To thank her. I thought she'd be here and I wanted her to see me well and strong because of her and I wanted to thank her.

HANNAH. Of course.

LISA. I didn't think for a moment…

HANNAH. You can still do it.

LISA. I really thought she was so strong.

HANNAH. You can still thank her.

LISA. I should go.

HANNAH. I still talk to her. So can you. It helps. I tell her what I feel about her. You can do that. Her energy is still in the room. I believe that. Do you believe that?

LISA. I don't know.

HANNAH. I can sense it. Can you see her?

LISA. Yes.

HANNAH. What does she look like?

LISA. Like she did that day.

HANNAH. How was that?

LISA. Like…a very beautiful woman. A guide. A helper.

HANNAH. She doesn't look ill to you?

LISA. No. Strong. Well.

HANNAH. What's she doing?

LISA. Sitting there. Listening to me.

HANNAH. Then tell her what you…thank her.

LISA. Yes.

LISA. Hello.

MERYL. Hello.

LISA. I'm sorry.

MERYL. You don't need to be.

LISA. But I am. Sorry. That you died and I lived. That's not fair.

MERYL. It's the way it is.

LISA. It shouldn't have been.

MERYL. I looked at you that morning and I thought: She's a very weak person and I'm a very strong person.

LISA. You were very frightened.

MERYL. Maybe.

LISA. Your own cancer was…it made you frightened. Forgive yourself.

MERYL. When all the time you were the stronger –

LISA. Lucky.

MERYL. You were strong and positive and I…

LISA. It's not like that.

MERYL. There are strong people who live. There are weak people who die.

LISA. No. We work on ourselves. We create ourselves, our thoughts make us –

MERYL. Blah blah.

LISA. You taught me that: you taught me that if we can find our anger, release our anger, forgive and move forward into a –

MERYL. BLAH. All lies.

LISA. But I'm the proof. I'm alive.

MERYL. I'm the proof. I'm dead. Nothing works. Nothing to be done. All the years I wasted on the mirrors and the drawings and the games, all –

LISA. You gave me life.

MERYL. Nothing to be done.

LISA. She says it was a spiritual moment. Beautiful. Your soul left your body.

MERYL. No. She can't hear. She's too young. I was screaming, crying out, cursing 'I hate this. I hate this. I hate this' …she couldn't hear it.

LISA. Is there peace now?

MERYL. No.

LISA. Surely you can find a bit of – ?

MERYL. Just…great anger because I lost the fight.

LISA. Are you angry with me?

MERYL. With you? No.

LISA. I came to thank you.

MERYL. You did the work on yourself.

LISA. But you were my guide. And now I have a life with – my girl is doing so well at school, we've bought a second place in France. We go there at the weekends. Everything has worked out so well. And that's all because of you. So thank you.

MERYL. It wasn't me.

LISA. I want you to accept my gratitude.

MERYL. I can't.

LISA. I need you – it's a closure for me – if you'll acknowledge how –

MERYL. I'll never do it.

LISA. All this blame, all this hatred you've got to do more work on yourself.

MERYL. You think so?

LISA. Oh yes. It never stops, the work on yourself. I'm well now but it doesn't mean I don't stop working on myself. Come and look at yourself in the mirror. What do you see?

MERYL. Nothing.

LISA. I can see you.

MERYL. There's nothing there.

LISA. Of course there is. It's you. You're beautiful and you're strong. Only you can love yourself. Only you can forgive yourself. Say: I love you and I forgive you.

MERYL. I can't.

LISA. I love you and I forgive you.

MERYL. No.

LISA. I love you and I forgive you.

MERYL. There's nothing there. I'm nobody. I'm nowhere. You have a life. Go on. Go back there.

LISA. But there's no closure for me unless you –

MERYL. I can't give you – didn't I give you enough? Didn't I give you life? I died and you – I won't accept your thanks. I won't forgive myself. I can't give you that.

LISA. But I can't live with the feeling that you – Can't you see? I feel as though I came here and I took your life. I feel as though I'm alive because you're – and I can't spend my days with that –

MERYL. Yes you will. You'll live with that. You'll carry on.

HANNAH. Did you thank her?

LISA. Yes I did.

HANNAH. And how was it?

LISA. It was… Very peaceful. Very calm. I told her that I had a wonderful life and I thanked her for her healing powers and it was very beautiful. She forgave herself and accepted my thanks. There's…

HANNAH. Closure?

LISA. Yes. There's a closure now.

HANNAH. Did she look beautiful and strong?

LISA. Oh yes. Very beautiful. Very strong. Thank you. I'm going now.

HANNAH. I see her.

LISA. Now?

HANNAH. Not now. No. But sometimes I see her and she… I can't see her like that… I see her and she's worn away. Her flesh is grey. Her gums are sore. Her eyes have no light in them. She has a tube in her arm and her nose. Catheter. She's like she was the day she passed on. I want to see something else but that's what she is when I see her.

LISA. Oh no. She isn't like that all.

HANNAH. No?

LISA. You've got that wrong. She's here now. She's very calm. She's very forgiving. She's forgiven everyone, you, me, the surgeons, everyone. And she's done the work on herself. She's forgiven herself. And she's beautiful. Can you see that?

HANNAH. No.

LISA. If you look, really look you can see that, can you see her?

HANNAH. Yes.

LISA. And how does she look?

HANNAH. Calm. Wise. Beautiful.

LISA. That's right. Isn't that great? Everything worked out for the best.

    (They are in silence.)

End